But Little Chick saw a delicious patch of weeds, and away he hopped...

"Yum-yum," cheeped Little Chick as he pecked at seeds, berries, and tasty shoots. But after a while...

...Little Chick looked around–he was all alone.
"Oh no," cheeped Little Chick, "I'm lost!" And
he hopped into the grass to look for his mother. But...

"Moo! Moo!" bellowed a bull. "What
are you doing in my meadow?"
"I've lost my mother," cheeped Little Chick.

"I saw someone by the fence," snorted the bull.
"It must be my mother," cheeped Little Chick,
and he hopped through the fence. But...

"Oink! Oink!" grunted three piglets.
"What are you doing in our field?"
"I've lost my mother," cheeped Little Chick.

"We heard someone moving in the bushes,"
squealed the piglets. So Little Chick hopped
into the undergrowth. But...

"Croak! Croak!" said a toad. "What
are you doing under my toadstool?"
"I've lost my mother," cheeped Little Chick.

"Someone brushed past me just a moment ago,"
croaked the toad. So Little Chick hopped past the
toad and into the brambles. But...

"Baa! Baa!" bleated some lambs. "What are you doing in our pasture?"
"I've lost my mother," cheeped Little Chick.

"We saw someone go into the wheat field," cried the lambs. So Little Chick hopped into the golden wheat. But...

"Squeak! Squeak!" called four field mice.
"What are you doing in this wheat field?"
"I've lost my mother," cheeped Little Chick.

"We just saw her go by," squeaked the mice.
"Hooray!" cheeped Little Chick, and he
hurried on. But...

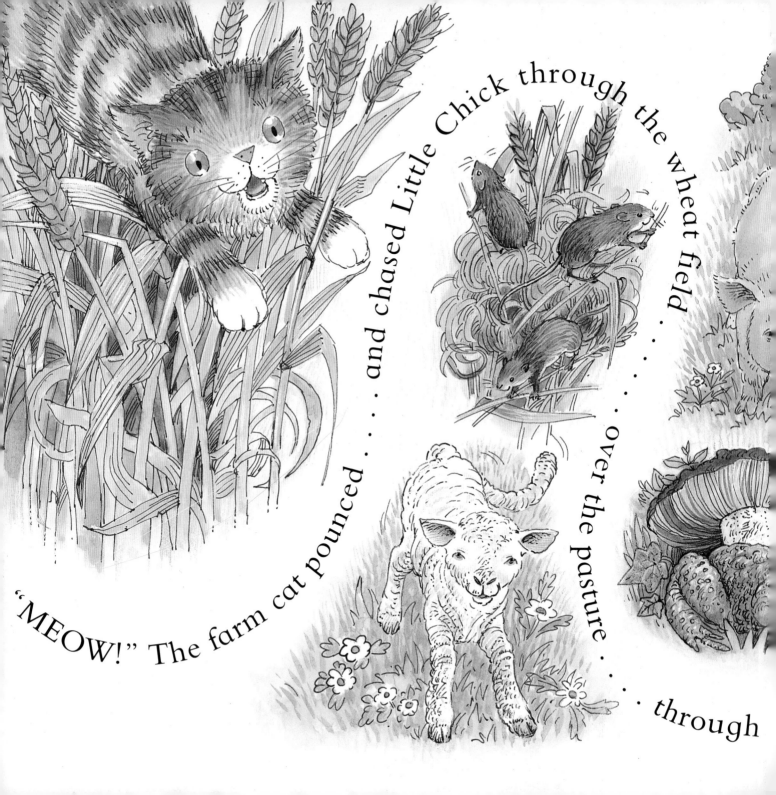

"MEOW!" The farm cat pounced . . . . . and chased Little Chick through the wheat field . . . . . . over the pasture . . . . . . through

the bushes ... over the field ... across the meadow ... all the way to the chicken coop

"Oh, there you are, Little Chick,"
clucked Mother Hen. "I was
looking for you everywhere..."